From Polio to Ironman

Thoughts about Life and Overcoming

2

Bjørn Rasmussen

From Polio to Ironman

Thoughts about Life and Overcoming

Contents

Preface 6

My Childhood in Aarhus......................................7

Moving to Kalundborg..10

Moving to Copenhagen and Ølstykke 12

Bicycling in the Ølstykke Bicycle Club 14

Bicycling in the Roskilde Bicycle Club.............15

Jogging in the Ølstykke Jogging Club..............17

Learning to Swim..20

Triathlon 21

Triathlon on the Ironman Distance 23

Ten years after 32

The Future 49

The Meaning of Life 52

Preface

I have written this book for myself. After being employed for 44 years I recently retired in 2002 and am deciding how to best use my new freedom. I will spend my time doing what I like to do and I will try to be happy.

This book is about surviving with polio, and I believe other polio survivors would like to read about my experiences to see that they, too, can live and thrive in spite of polio. My hope is that this book can help them to be happier and more content with life.

This book is also about making wishes come true. If you really want to be stronger, or more successful in life for that matter, you must believe in yourself. There are lots of obstacles—your own mind must not be one of them.

I was born December 18, 1941, during World War II. There was little food. My mother could not breast-feed me, so I was fed sugar water. It was very common to give babies sugar water at that time. My father, Ejnar, was a carpenter, and my mother, Ingeborg, was a bookbinder.

I got polio the first month I was born. There was a polio epidemic at that time and I became very sick. My condition was so bad, my parents told me later, that the doctors recommended letting me die. But my parents wanted me to live, and that is why I can write this book. The polio struck my left hip and left leg—my right hip and leg were OK.

I was at the hospital for a month. Then I came home to my parents. As far as I remember, there was no rehabilitation. How do you rehabilitate a baby? Once a year I went back to the hospital to see if my left leg was getting weaker. It was always the same, I think. The doctors didn't tell me anything since I was only a child.

The polio killed some of the nerves in my left hip and leg, leaving me with very little muscle power on my left side—only 10% compared to my right side.

The lack of strength in my left leg became a problem when I was old enough to go to school. The school was three stories high with lots of stairs up and down. I didn't like stairs. I had to use my strong right leg when I climbed the stairs—my weak left leg just dragged behind.

I also discovered I was terrible in gymnastics. Because of the polio I couldn't do the various jumps, and I was a very bad runner.

I remember a sports day in fifth grade. There were four boys on each running team. The two strongest boys on my team dragged me the whole route. It was very hard and frustrating being a dead weight and hurting, rather than helping, my teammates. I knew they could have won without me.

I was good at something, however. I was the best in my class at climbing a rope. Here I could use the muscles in my arms, and we weren't supposed to use our legs anyway. I was also good at pulling my legs to my chin when I was on the top wall bar, because I had good muscles in my abdomen.

Soccer was the favorite sport of my class, but I was the lousiest soccer player. Yet I can remember one day, to everyone's surprise, when I scored two goals. I felt ecstatic. It only happened that one day, but I will never forget it. It was some kind of magic, and I knew that if this could happen, anything could happen.

I rode my bicycle every day with my friends. In fact, I rode my bicycle much better than I ran. When I ran, I could only go as fast as my weaker left leg, which had only 10% the strength of my right leg. When biking, however, my strong right leg determined how fast I could go. It made a big difference.

My best friend, Knud, lived on the same street as I did growing up. He was a stout boy, but I could just keep up with him on a bicycle. We made many fine bicycle rides to the beach to look at girls. Later on, Knud immigrated to the United States. Today he has a bar at Key West, Florida. I am almost sure I could still keep up with him on a bicycle.

After 10 years of education I left school. (In Denmark at that time, most youth went to school for eight years—those who wanted to work with their hands. For people who wanted to work in an office, 10 years of school was necessary, along with learning the foreign languages of English, German and French.) I was displeased with my grade in physical education, which was a D. This one grade pulled my total examination results down and made it difficult for me to find a job. I complained to the gym master, but he simply asked me, "Do you think you deserve more worth than a D?" While I had to admit that I didn't deserve anything better, I was still very disappointed and discontented.

Moving to Kalundborg

Despite my D in physical education, my total overall grade was a B+ and was sufficient to get me a job with the Customs Administration. Why did I want to work at the Customs Administration? My father recommended it. Sometimes he worked as a carpenter at the customhouse of Aarhus, a nearby city. He told me that the staff took it very easy there and that the work wasn't as hard as being a carpenter. So I got a job at Kalundborg Custom House and worked there for two years.

I was still lame because of the polio. To reduce the limping I had to add an extra inch (2 cm) to the sole of my left shoe. The shoemaker in Kalundborg told me that in my case, the government would pay for a pair of handmade shoes. I liked to hear that. He measured my legs and added an extra inch and a quarter (3 cm) inside the sole of my left shoe.

I soon found out that this was a big mistake. I felt like I was wearing a high-heeled shoe on my left foot and a normal shoe on my right foot. I don't know why I used those shoes. I think it was because I was told that they were very expensive. They lasted two years before I threw them out with the garbage. I went back to my old system of wearing normal shoes with an extra sole added beneath my left shoe.

When you think about your self-esteem, especially as a teenager, it's important that your shoes look alike.

(Today I only buy normal shoes with enough room in the left shoe for an extra sole. The extra sole is now about a half-inch thick (1 cm).

Moving to Copenhagen and Ølstykke

After working hard and becoming a skilled customs officer, I was transferred to Copenhagen. I worked at many different places there, often only a month at each place. I always rode my bicycle from my home to my office. It was the best exercise for me.

In the evenings I trained weightlifting. I was very slender and couldn't lift much. But I liked training with weights. My body became stronger and it gave a boost to my self-confidence.

I married Charlotte ("Lotte") September 5, 1964. We got a son, Martin, on February 18, 1965. We lived in a small house at Østerbro for two years. At that time I trained with weights at Østerbro Stadium. The training did not make me any bigger physically, but I liked it.

In 1966 we moved to Ølstykke, where we still live today. We played tennis, badminton and table tennis, but nothing really serious.

Martin went to school in Ølstykke, and one of his friends was a member of the Ølstykke Bicycle Club. Martin wanted to join the club, but he was a little shy and wanted me to go with him. The year was 1978. We joined the club at the square in Ølstykke. Twenty-five other boys and one girl, all his age, were there, and I whispered to Martin, "It doesn't look too difficult. We can easily follow these kids!"

The bicycle tours were 3-5 miles (5-8 km) long. After riding only a mile and a quarter (2 km), Martin and I were all by ourself. All of the others, including the little girl, had disappeared far in front of us, and we could not catch them. But we did not give up. The next week we joined them again, and each time we participated we became a little bit stronger.

Bicycling in the Ølstykke Bicycle Club

I was a member of the Ølstykke Bicycle Club for a couple of years. And suddenly we did not train with the children, but with grown ups. It was hard. We bought expensive bicycles with Campagnolo Record equipment. Martin became stronger and stronger. He could easily follow the others. It was more difficult for me. The tours were now 30-60 miles long (50-100 km). Normally we rode out with the wind against us and biked homeward with the wind behind us.

Martin soon developed other interests, but I continued riding with the bike club. I trained hard and earned my license from the Bicycle Union to compete in "real" races against other professional bicyclists. I participated in three to four really hard races, but of course I did not win anything.

The last day I trained with the Ølstykke Bicycle Club was for a tour going to Gilleleje and back. The ride to Gilleleje was unusually quick because we had the wind behind us. I got tired in Gilleleje, however, and had to bike home all alone the last 30 miles (50 km) with the wind against me. I got so mad for being so far behind that I resigned my membership.

I did not cry over quitting the Ølstykke Bicycle Club because I had already started training in another bicycle club in Roskilde.

In 1979 Lotte and I started to ride in the Roskilde Bicycle Club's section for veterans. The club had an A, B and C team. We trained Wednesday and Sunday, always starting from Roskilde Square. About 30-40 bicyclists came every time.

In the beginning we both joined the slower C team. They were very social, and always waited if someone was tired. I liked that. But after a couple of tours with the C team, I joined the B team.

The B team was the right team for me. I felt very strong here. The tours were 30-60 miles (50-100 km) long.

Lotte and I participated in some big bicycle races for veterans. Even though these races included "amateurs," they were quite grueling. The course for the Vättern Rundan race in Sweden circled Vättern Lake. It was 188 miles (300 km) long and had 6,500 participants. The Sjælland Rundt race in Denmark was 197 miles (315 km) long and had 1,500 participants.

As the training continued I became better and better and joined the A team. Almost all of the members were racing cyclists with racing licenses. I was on the A team for about one year, but it was very difficult. I just was not strong enough.

I remember one day when I had been riding fast for hours and suddenly got cramps in my legs. It was so painful I had to jump off my bike. I was lying on the road and could not move. I could not stand up. Whatever I did I got more cramps. I had cramps in all my leg muscles. After laying for five minutes on the road, my friends came by, lifted me up on the bicycle and pushed me home.

I trained daily on my bicycle, but it was not enough. What could I do to become a better racing cyclist? I figured I could be better on my bicycle if I started jogging one or two times every week. So I started jogging with Lotte a few minutes three times a week. It was fun.

Our runs became longer and longer.

Then we joined a runners club in Ølstykke. Every Saturday we ran about six miles (10 km) together with other joggers. This kind of training was really good—so good, in fact, that I was tired the day after and couldn't keep up with the A team on the Sunday bicycle tours.

Jogging in the Ølstykke Jogging Club

(1982-1994)

Every Saturday we met at the Jørlunde schoolyard to run. The hardest-training members of the jogging club ran every day of the week, but all of the members ran on Saturdays. There were 25-30 joggers in the Ølstykke Jogging Club.

Every Saturday I ran a little longer. I entered competitions jogging three or six miles (five or ten kilometers). Yes, I even ran in the 8.2 mile (13.2 km) "Eremitageløb." My personal record at the Eremitageløb was one hour and twelve minutes. Because I remembered being such a bad runner when I was in school, I became euphoric with joy because I finally realized I really could run. I was not as fast as the average man in my age group, but I was faster than the average woman for my age. When someone asked me how fast I could run I answered, "I run excellent for a woman my age!" Lotte, on the other hand, ran faster than the average man for her age.

Later on we started to run half marathons, which are 13.1 miles (21 km) long. I had my personal best record for the half marathon in 1991: 1 hour and 52 minutes.

But most of the half marathons took me two hours.

My biggest dream at that time was to run a full marathon— 26.2 miles (42.2 km) long. I imagined that if I, someone with polio, could run a marathon, then I would be just as good as any other "normal" runner. I figured it would really strengthen my self-esteem.

In 1988 I participated in the Wonderful Copenhagen marathon. My times for this year and the years following in this and other marathons were:

Marathon	Time	Place
1988 Wonderful Copenhagen	5 hours, 53 mins	Second to the last
1989 Wonderful Copenhagen	5 hours, 9 mins	
1990 Wonderful Copenhagen	4 hours, 41 mins	My personal best
1991 Wonderful Copenhagen	4 hours, 43 mins	
1991 Holger Danske	4 hours, 59 mins	Last
1992 Wonderful Copenhagen	5 hours, 2 mins	
1993 Wonderful Copenhagen	5 hours, 12 mins	
1994 Wonderful Copenhagen	5 hours, 6 mins	

Lotte participated in all of the above marathons as well. She always reached the finish line a couple of hours before me. Her personal record is 3 hours, 20 minutes.

Although I trained a lot, I could not keep up with the other members of the jogging club. It was frustrating to start each Saturday with 30 other runners and only be able to follow them for three-tenths of a mile (0.5 km).

And then I ran alone for the next 6-9 miles (10-15 km). That was why I got a dog, for company. It was a borzoi, and his name was Aron. He was a good companion on my running tours. A borzoi is a greyhound, which can run very fast. Aron had no problem keeping up with me when I ran ;o).

Because Lotte and I both trained on our bicycles and jogged, it seemed natural to think about participating in a triathlon where you run, bike and swim. At least I could try it. My problem, however, was that I could not swim. I would have to learn to swim first.

Learning to Swim

We joined the „Laksen" Swim Club in Ølstykke. Because our goal was to participate in a triathlon, I knew I'd have to learn to swim a long distance and do it fast. Knowing that the crawl was a faster swimming stroke than the breaststroke, I decided to learn to do the crawl.

Until now the longest distance I could swim was doing the breaststroke 25 meters (27 yards) in the public indoor pool (svoemmehal, which means "swimming hall"). And now, at 50 years old, I had to learn to do the crawl. Experts told me that people over 40 years old couldn't learn to crawl correctly. I found out this wasn't true—but it takes a long time to learn.

It took me more than three months to learn to swim 25 meters doing the crawl without a break. But the week after I could swim 50 meters (54 yards) and suddenly there was no limit. I could go on and on. The longest distance I swam was 6.2 miles (10 km) in the Ølstykke swimming pool. It wasn't that difficult, but it did take a lot of time. The hardest thing about swimming is to learn to swim fast. You must have a good swimming style to swim fast.

In the swim club I learned life-saving and diving skills. The other swimmers trained to pass the life-saving test. Since my goal wasn't to pass that test, I just swam up and down the lanes.

Triathlon

My first triathlon was with the Roskilde Bicycle Club in 1987. There was a 0.3-mile (500 m) swim, a 28-mile (45 km) bicycle ride and a 4.7-mile (7.5 km) run. Only twelve people participated. At that time I was only able to swim 25 meters, and therefore I said that I would participate if I was allowed to swim along one of the two sides of the pool.

They did not remember my request, and suddenly I was in the middle of the pool where I would start the swim.   There was a floating rope between each lane. I thought I could cling to this rope when I got tired.

I jumped into the pool and rested on the rope many times during the long swim. All the others finished the swim before me. My bicycle ride and my jogging were OK, but I came in last. I really hate to come in last, and I decided to do better the next time.

I participated in the following triathlons:

Year	Triathlon	Swim (miles/ km)	Bicycle (miles/ km)	Run (miles/k m)	Results for age group
1988	Hørsholm	0.25 mi/ 0.4 km	12.2 mi/ 19.6 km	2.5 mi/ 4 km	19 out of 24
1988	Arresø	0.31 mi/ 0.5 km	14.6 mi/ 23.5 km	4.3 mi/ 6.9 km	94 out of 104
1988	Hillerød	0.62 mi/ 1.0 km	48.5 mi/ 78 km	13 mi/ 21 km	156 out of 195
1989	Hørsholm	0.25 mi/ 0.4 km	12.2 mi/ 19.6 km	2.5 mi/ 4 km	21 out of 33
1989	Arresø	0.31 mi/ 0.5 km	14.6 mi/ 23.5 km	4.3 mi/ 6.9 km	27 out of 38
1989	Blovstrød	0.31 mi/ 0.5 km	19.3 mi/ 31 km	5.3 mi/ 8.5km	10 out of 15
1989	Hillerød	0.62 mi/ 1.0 km	48.5 mi/ 78 km	13 mi/ 21 km	134 out of 186
1990	Hørsholm	0.25 mi/ 0.4 km	12.2 mi/ 19.6 km	2.5 mi/ 4 km	201 out of 255
1990	Køge	0.31 mi/ 0.5 km	16.8 mi/ 27 km	5.9 mi/ 9.5 km	36 out of 63
1990	Holbæk	0.93 mi/ 1.5 km	24.9 mi/ 40 km	6.2 mi/ 10 km	16 out of 17
1990	Hillerød	0.62 mi/ 1.0 km	48.5 mi/ 78 km	13 mi/ 21 km	41 out of 62
1991	Køge	0.31 mi/ 0.5 km	16.8 mi/ 27 km	5.9 mi/ 9.5 km	8 out of 13
1991	Holbæk	0.93 mi/ 1.5 km	24.9 mi/ 40 km	6.2 mi/ 10 km	3 out of 5
1992	Brøndby	0.93 mi/ 1.5 km	24.9 mi/ 40 km	6.2 mi/ 10 km	84 out of 101
1992	Sorø	0.6 mi/ 0.95 km	30 mi/ 45 km	6.5 mi/ 10.5 km	40 out of 49

In August 1991 Lotte and I signed up for the Rødekro Ironman competition. The Ironman is a triathlon with distances that are much longer. My training in 1991, with total miles trained for each event by month, was as follows:

Month	Swim (miles/ km)	Bicycle (miles/ km)	Run (miles/ km)
January	18.6 mi/ 30 km	350 mi/ 564 km	155 mi/ 250 km
February	16.8 mi/ 27 km	293 mi/ 472 km	171 mi/ 275 km
March	16.2 mi/ 26 km	527 mi/ 848 km	204 mi/ 329 km
April	22.4 mi/ 36 km	508 mi/ 817 km	226 mi/ 364 km
May	11.2 mi/ 18 km	441 mi/ 709 km	183 mi/ 295 km
June	11.8 mi/ 19 km	524 mi/ 843 km	144 mi/ 232 km
July	28 mi/ 45 km	1,214 mi/ 1,953 km	168 mi/ 271 km
Total	125 mi/ 201 km	3,858 mi/ 6,208 km	1,254 mi/ 2,018 km

Since my longest swim to this point was 6.2 miles (10 km), I was not afraid of the swimming distance. And I am a fast swimmer for my age. But I was afraid of getting cramps during the swim. That was why I trained a great deal swimming in open water. I had also trained a lot on my bicycle and was not afraid of the distance. To prepare for the long run, I had jogged an average of 6.2 miles (10 km) each day and had jogged 18.6 miles (30 km) a couple of times. I had always started my training on my bicycle or by swimming first, sometimes doing all three things on the same day. I was most afraid of the marathon distance. I did not know if I could do it after the swim and the bicycle ride.

I made a T-shirt to wear during the marathon that said, "Polio 1941 - Ironman 1991," (but I never used it.)

The night before the contest we stayed in a youth hostel in a 6-person room. But I had a huge problem. I could not sleep. All night I was sweating all over. I had no sleeping pills. I did not sleep even five minutes all night.

The next morning I felt as tired as if I had already jogged a half marathon (13 miles). This was a bad start. But now I was here. I had trained hard for half a year. I would not give up before I had started.

On August 10, 1991, at 7:00 in the morning, we stood in the 70-degree water (21 degrees Celsius) to begin the swimming portion of the Ironman.

After swimming only 0.6 mile (1 km) I had cramp. It never disappeared. After swimming 1.9 miles (3 km) the cramps were so strong that I had to quit. A boat came.

They took me out from the water and brought me back to the beach.

Even though I was out of the contest, I wanted to ride the 112 miles (180 km) on my bicycle to test if I could run after that, even if it were only a few miles. Furthermore, it would take 13 hours before I could expect Lotte back from her run, and I couldn't just sit down in the grass and wait all that time.

I got on my bike and rode the 112 miles, but when I got off and tried to run, I couldn't run even one yard.

Lotte finished both the swim and the bike ride, but she felt too tired to start running the marathon, especially when she heard that I had given up. She is so wise. She knew I would be hard to deal with if she was the only one who had finished the contest.

After this experience we really wanted the title of Ironman and signed up for the contest scheduled for the next year on August 8, 1992.

My training in 1992 was as follows:

Month	Swim (miles/ km)	Bicycle (miles/ km)	Run (miles/ km)
January	18 mi/ 29 km	104 mi/ 131 km	104 mi/ 167 km
February	16.2 mi/ 26 km	275 mi/ 442 km	105 mi/ 169 km
March	19.3 mi/ 31 km	245 mi/ 395 km	116 mi/ 187 km

April	16.8 mi/ 27 km	148 mi/ 238 km	140 mi/ 226 km
May	9.9 mi/ 16 km	280 mi/ 451 km	183 mi/ 295 km
June	20.5 mi/ 33 km	783 mi/ 1,260 km	139 mi/ 223 km
July	24.9 mi/ 40 km	897 mi/ 1,444 km	111 mi/ 178 km
Total	126 mi/ 202 km	2,710 mi/ 4,361 km	900 mi/ 1,449 km

My training on the bicycle and jogging in 1992 was only 70% of my training the year before. Why train so much, I thought, if I end up stopping the competition during the swim because of cramps? I experimented with different things to see if I could avoid the cramps while swimming.

I had for some time been taking a herbal medicine called Gingko Biloba, which was recommended for elderly people to avoid cramps at night. Sounded like the right thing for me. And I ate a lot of vitamins and minerals, especially magnesium.

When I swam in cold water for a long time, however, there was still a chance I could get cramps. The last thing I came up with (one week before the contest) was to wear a thick woolen undershirt and three pairs of woolen underwear under my wetsuit, all washed in lanolin. This really helped to keep me warm.

The swim

On August 6, 1992, at 7:00 in the morning, the water was only 64 degrees (18 degrees Celsius). We had to swim 1.2 miles (1900 meters) two times around, a total of 2.4 miles.

Before the swim. Lotte and I are just in front of the three flags.

The first 1.2 miles (1900 meters) went fine, but then my legs began to feel strange and I knew I would have to be careful. My thighs vibrated, even though I tried to relax. Fortunately nothing happened, and I continued to swim. But it was with frayed nerves because of the vibrating in my thighs. Every yard I swam I was afraid I would get cramps. But it never happened, and it was with great relief that I made it back to shore. My swim took 1 hour and 20 minutes, and the rest of the contest was pure holiday I thought. I was euphoric after having finished the swim. I was going to take one thing at a time.

27

The Bicycle Tour

The area where the athletes changed from swimsuits to cycle attire had no room for a man like me who walked slowly, both to get his bicycle and to change clothes. All around me people ran, stumbled and cursed. I enjoyed the scene, and I enjoyed the fact that the worst was past me. I thought about what clothes I should wear now for the 112-mile bike ride (180 km)—long or short cycle trousers? Long or short sleeves? Underwear or rain jacket? The weather was dark, and it was raining a little.

Most of the other men jumped on their bicycle only with swimming trunks and with something that looked like a bra, which is why I chose short cycle trousers, underwear and a blouse with long sleeves. Later on it proved to be a good choice. The men who passed me on the course did not have to ring a bell. When they were still a long distance away I could hear their chattering teeth.

Well, I was up on my bike and rode the beautiful 112 miles (180 km) all by myself. Being a lousy runner in the first place, and because it was hard for me to run after a long ride on the bicycle, I decided to bike at a pace that did not make me tired. I could do this for the first 31 miles (50 km) because the wind was at my back. But then the wind turned against me for the next 28 miles (45 km), and if I didn't keep pedaling the bike stood still. I tried to go at a quiet pace, but it was not easy. Like the swim, we had to go through the same route two times. Late in the route, Lotte passed me and told me she had overtaken a lot of athletes. That was music to my ears.

I was on my bike for 7 hours and 36 minutes. My average speed was 15 miles (24 km) an hour.

The Marathon

It felt good to get off the bike. I thought, Now I am almost through. I just have to change clothes and run 26.2 miles (42 km). And the spectators will cheer me up and make it easy for me.

We had to run the 6.6-mile (10.55-km) route four times, each time running through a stadium. I started the run with Lotte and kept up with her for about 10 seconds. It was cheerful indeed, as long as it lasted.

The race volunteers gave me two cups of Isostar (an energy drink), because I thought I needed more of a boost than common water could give me. Unfortunately, those cups made my stomach hurt. I was told later that the Isostar was far too strong—I should have chosen water.

I had problems with my stomach for the first 6.2 miles(10 km), but at least I could run most of the time. I was satisfied.

There were lots and lots of runners. Half of them looked extremely fresh. The "fresh" runners were the ones who participated in a relay race. The father swam, the mother biked and junior ran. The individuals who did everything—the swimming, bicycling and now running—looked miserable.

My second time around I walked some and ran some. I was happy when I was through with the first 13.1 miles (21 km)— half of the marathon—in just two hours.

To be an Ironman you must complete the entire race within 16 hours. I had already used 12 hours up to this point and many athletes had finished. I was tired and afraid of being injured if I continued to run. I thought my best chance was to walk. Besides, I had plenty of time.

My long walk began as I started the third lap around the course, which turned out to be easy. There were still many athletes on the route and every few miles (3 km) I could get water, fruit and bread, and a talk with the helpers.

Approximately 3,000 people lived in Rødekro, 600 of which helped at this Ironman. They were nice people, and I said thanks and goodbye to all the helpers my last lap (6.2 miles) around. Only a couple of runners were behind me, and it was getting dark.

The worst thing now was that the last 1.9 miles (3 km) went through a dark forest with no lights. I had to go slow as I could not see where I was stepping.

The highlight of the day came when I saw the stadium with lots of lights. There were plenty of happy people, and Lotte gave me a bunch of flowers that she had received herself earlier.

I made it in 15 hours, 56 minutes. I was happy that I was not the last person. Two people came in after me. They made it in 16 hours, too.

It was a great experience, but I will not do it again.

At the finish line. Lotte got a bronze medal in her age group. She was satisfied, too. Her time was 13 hours, 44 minutes.

Running with my dogs

Why do I run? Man is made to run. Long ago running was necessary to survive. You use your muscles far more running than walking. My intention is to run every day. Sometimes I am tired and I want to sit in my chair in front of the television. I think the Holy Bible says somewhere that our spirit is strong, but our flesh is weak. You want to run, but you are too tired to do it.

I do not ask myself, "Shall I run today, or am I too tired?" Rather, I say, "How far shall I run today?" If I am very tired I only run 0.3 of a mile (0.5 km). Normally I run at least 0.62 of a mile (1.0 km).

Of course I don't run if it really hurts. But if my muscles ache a little or I'm a little tired I can still run. It's common knowledge that it's good to run a little the day after a marathon. (Maybe a little like taking a beer the day after a drinking bout if you've got a headache.)

I like running with my dogs; we have a good talk and I get my problems solved. I have three dogs. Lady, an English setter, is eight years old. And Boris and Babuska, brother and sister, were born May 4, 2001. Boris and Babuska are borzois—greyhounds. I walk or run with them one at a time, which is when they are most polite to other dogs. Together they are a pack of wolves. I don't want that.

My first borzoi was Aron. I got him when he was two years old. He was a good male dog. Not many borzois are seen in Denmark.

Lotte and Aron

Aron was very friendly to people and to female dogs. But as a very dominating male dog he wanted to show other male dogs that he was the biggest and the strongest. He never did hurt another dog, though.

There is something strange about a male dog. It likes most of the other male dogs, but suddenly there is one it does not like. Humans don't understand this. We try and try to figure out which dog he will like but we often guess wrong.

A borzoi does not need as much exercise as you might think. My English setter, Lady, wants to walk all the time. It's different with a borzoi. It likes to sleep in the sofa all day. Most of the times I went with Lady, Aron wanted to stay home on the sofa.

Aron was with me when I went jogging, however. I don't run fast. If I start with other joggers they soon disappear in the horizon. But Aron always stayed with me. When he died at eight years old I felt alone. I still had Lady, but she is mostly Lotte's dog.

I managed without a borzoi for half a year. Then one night I woke up and missed my borzoi so much that I started looking on the Internet for a borzoi puppy. I found only one borzoi litter, but when I looked at the pictures I had to get one of those puppies. There were three males and a female.

Having a female already, Lady, I thought it best to get a borzoi female. Next day I bought the borzoi puppy. Her name was Babuska, which means "Grandma" in Russian. Soon it became best friends with Lady. But Lady was an older dog, and not so fond of playing with Babuska all the time.

Babuska became an extremely good dog. She was so nice and kind that I wanted to do everything to make her happy. That was why I soon bought one of her brothers she liked so much from the same litter. His name was Boris. Babuska and Boris are best friends, and I like to see them play. They are always together.

When Babuska and Boris play together, it looks as if they are biting each other in the neck and throat. It looks dangerous, but is quite harmless. They fight like skilled karate fighters, who kick each other without hurting each other at all. They know exactly how far they can go without hurting each other.

When Boris meets another dog he rushes at it just like he does when playing with Babuska. Dog owners who don't know him don't like this kind of wild playing. The dogs normally do not care. But the owners!!! That is why I normally have Boris on a leash when we meet other dogs he does not know. Not because of the dogs, but because of the owners who always seem to fear the worst. I understand how they feel, especially since Boris is a huge dog.

Boris and Babuska dancing

Why am I so fond of borzois? My English setter is just as good a dog to run with, maybe better. Lady does not care about the dogs we meet. Her only interest is birds, especially blackbirds. When I walk with Lady we talk about the blackbirds we meet. Lady likes most to walk close to the private hedges, where the blackbirds sit. Twilight is the best time because the blackbirds want to go asleep in the hedges. Then Lady and I sneak along the hedges to see if we can make a blackbird fly. I pity the bird that wants to sleep, but Lady loves this game.

I like the borzois because they are so beautiful and full of grace, like no other dog. They are very swift. Maybe because I've had polio and want to be swift myself is the reason I admire the borzoi—they have the swiftness I do not have.

When my borzois are playing they run so fast that I have to stand still. If they run towards me and I move in the wrong direction, it could be dangerous for me. I never let them play when children are around. They ask, "Do they bite?" "No," I say. "They do not bite, but it is dangerous if they run into you".

My borzois have never run into anybody. They take evasive action or jump over whatever is in the way. On television I have seen a borzoi jump higher than five feet (1.6 meters). Even so, a person who at the last moment walks to the wrong side is difficult to avoid.

My car

I like swift and beautiful cars as well as swift and beautiful dogs. That is why I bought a 1977 Porsche 911. It was 25 years old in 2002. But I like to look at my car. I find it beautiful. And I like to hear the deep roar of the engine. It sounds exactly like Boris growling.

Like the borzoi, the Porsche is extremely fast and beautiful—qualities I would like to have myself. Perhaps a psychologist would be interested in this information about me.

I do not drive fast in my Porsche. Just knowing that the car is fast is enough for me. I have a garage in my garden where the Porsche can be protected during the winter. But I don't like to keep it where I can't see it. I want it in my carport, outside the window at my door, so I can enjoy looking at it all the time. It's like a piece of art. I do not drive it during the winter, but I want to enjoy its beauty—just like I enjoy looking at my borzois.

Boris ready to take the Porsche out for a spin.

There is no doubt that my interest in my borzois and my Porsche say something about me. Because I have had polio I want to be swift and beautiful myself, instead of slow and lame. I believe humans want to be perfect in soul and body. That is what we aim for in our inner thoughts.

Squats
What is the current strength in my legs today?

Excercise	Left leg	Right leg	Left leg % of right leg
Standing up lifting one leg back (leg curl)	2.2 lbs./ 1 kg	19.8 lbs./ 9 kg	11%
Lying on bench on stomach doing leg curl	4.4 lbs./ 2 kg	44 lbs./ 20 kg	10%
Sitting on bench doing a leg extension	37.5 lbs./ 17 kg	88 lbs./ 40 kg	43%
Lying on the floor on my back with stretched leg lifting the leg	4.4 lbs./ 2 kg	22 lbs./ 10 kg	20%
Lying on the floor on my back with my knee on my stomach lifting the leg (leg extension)	4.4 lbs./ 2 kg	24.3 lbs./ 11 kg	18%
Doing leg press with leg press machine	106 lbs./ 48 kg	276 lbs./ 125 kg	38%

The muscles I use doing a leg curl are the same I use when running. This means my weak left leg only has 11% of the strength of my right leg when I run. And because it is the weak leg that determines how fast you can run, I can only run slowly.

The muscles I use doing leg extensions are the same muscles I use when I am riding my bicycle. The strength of these muscles in my weak leg is 43% of the strength in my stronger right leg. But because it is the strong leg that determines the speed of the bicycle, my weaker left leg doesn't hinder me as much on the bike.

My left leg is approximately three quarters of an inch (2 cm) shorter than my right leg. My left thigh has a circumference of 14.2 inches (36 centimeters). My right thigh has a circumference of 20.5 inches (52 centimeters). The circumference of my left calf is 10.2 inches (26 centimeters); the circumference of my right calf is 13.4 inches (34 centimeters).

Having had polio, any wish for perfection is mostly concerned about reducing my disability. And if you believe that you are getting stronger, then you will be happier. I do not think the important thing is that you are actually getting stronger; it's more important that you believe you are getting stronger.

The best way to strengthen your legs, in my opinion, is to do squats. On the Internet I have read lots of things about Chi Kung. Squats can cure many illnesses. The first time I read this I didn't believe it. But after reading about people who claimed to be cured because they had been doing 100 squats every day, I started to wonder. I started doing squats myself.

For five months I did 100 squats every evening before I went to sleep. When I first started I was determined to do 100 squats every day for 100 days. The exercise said, "Do 100 squats every day for 100 days. If you forget to do the 100 squats even one day you will have to start all over again." On day number 85 I forgot to do my squats. I woke up at night, however, and did my 100 squats. I did not want to start all over again. I continued doing 100 squats every day, even when I had passed the first 100 days.

Right now I do 25 squats daily. Why only 25? Because 25 squats only takes a short time and I like to do them. One hundred squats takes a long time and makes me sweat all over so that I have to change clothes afterwards. Those 100 squats were so hard for me to do that most of the time I waited until just before going to bed to do them.

Many years ago I bought a leg press machine from a closed down fitness centre. It's a big thing—8 feet x 6 feet (2.5m x 1.8m). My wife hated to have it in the house. Now it's in the garage in the garden.

The leg press machine is good for training hard without getting injuries. Before this I trained doing squats with a barbell on my neck. But as my strong leg is four times stronger than my weak leg, I tend to do the press almost entirely with my strong leg, risking injury to my back.

I lie on my back in the leg press machine and press up with my legs. I normally press 220 pounds (100 kg). As I weigh only 132 pounds (60 kg), I have to work hard when using it. Currently I use the leg press machine three times a week, only doing five to ten lifts at a time.

I think it is very important to be able to relax. After I have increased my pulse by doing squats or leg presses (or running), I relax well and my heart rate is lowered.

Athletes normally have a low resting heart rate. When the body works hard it can relax well. And it is very important to relax if you want a healthy body and a healthy soul.

Yoga

I have always been interested in yoga, especially hathayoga. Every day I do the headstand (sirhasana), the shoulder stand (sarvangasana), the plough posture (halasana), the leg stretch (paschimotana), and the twist posture (Ardha Matsyendrasana). These five asanas take five minutes to do.

Years ago I did many more asanas, but it took a lot of time. Now I do the asanas I like. Of course, many readers will say I need to do some of the very important asanas. But everybody has to make a choice, and my choice is to do the five asanas just mentioned.

Chi Kung

Chi Kung is a lot of things. It's a Chinese system of medical science, a form of martial arts, spiritual exercises and much more. Yoga is one kind of Chi Kung, squats is another kind of Chi Kung. Karate and Kung fu are also part of Chi Kung.

I have don Tai Chi for some years now. Tai Chi is known as moving meditation. But it is also an old Chinese self-defense system. Doing Tai Chi is claimed to be curative, and I believe it. The first year I learned the common form of Tai Chi, which is very, very slow. Later on I learned a quick form of Tai chi.

I took up karate the same time I was learning Tai chi, but it was difficult to practice them both. After comparing the two, my favorite was karate.

Karate was more my style. Maybe the Tai chi is healthier, but I compare Tai chi to yoga. The Tai chi I learned was not much good for self defense, and the participants were mostly older women who were of the opinion that Tai chi could be used for self defense. I think it was fine they developed more self-confidence doing Tai chi, but I thought my time was better used learning karate.

Karate

I have only been in a real fight once in my life. I had just started school and was six years old. My classmates set up a fight between me and another boy. The other boy got a little nosebleed, but nobody got hurt.

When my wife and I finished the Ironman in 1992, we agreed that we would not do triathlons anymore. But then what? My wife had a colleague who had a black belt in Shotokan Karate. He was very enthusiastic about karate and persuaded her to start. She asked me to start too, and I said yes at once. Here was a sport that could give me more self-confidence. I told the karate instructor I was weak in one leg because of polio, and asked him if I could still do karate. He said that I could if I wanted to.

So in 1993 we started karate, at first in common clothes together with 20 other students. The other students were 20 years old on average, and I was 51 years old. Some had been doing karate earlier; kick boxing or Thai boxing. Some came just to fight. It was a hard time for me. One of the youngest students had trained in many kinds of martial arts before, and I did not like to train with him because he kicked very hard. Lotte and I agreed to continue until the first graduation. Then we could discuss about whether to stop or continue.

We bought a white karate gi (loose-fitting uniform) with a white belt, and after graduation we received an orange belt. So we continued. A lot of the young students stopped training. The rough guy stopped after one year. Our class got smaller and smaller and was finally put together with another class. We got green belt, and later violet belt, and we hoped for the brown belt.

Time passed by and we continued to train until one day we had the brown belt (3 kyu). And we wanted to continue a little longer.

The belts have the following value, white being the lowest:

White: 10 kyu
Yellow: 9 kyu
Orange: 8 kyu
Green: 7 og 6 kyu
Violet: 5 og 4 kyu
Brown: 3, 2 og 1 kyu

Each kyu could be done in half a year, and half a year later we were brown belts 2 kyu. Later we became1 kyu, which is the highest rank before the black belt. Lotte trained five years but did not want to fight for the black belt. She had nothing to prove. She stopped karate and trained Tai chi instead.

Lotte and I training while Lady looks on

I continued with karate. I had something to prove. I wanted to be just as good, maybe even better than the others, in spite of having had polio. Like the marathon and triathlon "the polio" drove me forward. I trained three evenings every week for some years.

In January 1999 I was allowed to try to graduate to the black belt. It was a weekend camp, and a high-ranking Japanese master was there, together with two high-ranking Danish senseis (teachers). We had to train all Saturday and Sunday morning. The graduation would take place Sunday afternoon.

I was tempted to only participate part of the time to conserve my strength, but I was told the Japanese master noticed who was there and who was not. My choice was to participate in everything and maybe be tired for the graduation test, or cheat a little with the training and have all my strength for graduation. I chose the first and trained all day Saturday with almost no breaks.

The graduation test was tough. We started with kihon, to show that we had mastered a lot of different punches and kicks. I am not good at kicks because it is difficult for me to keep my balance on my weak leg while I am kicking with the other leg. But I got through this part of the test.

After that the master took a pencil and placed it between two loose fingers. I was told to punch at the pencil with full power just enough to touch it a little, little bit. But if I punched the pencil out of his hand— goodbye and come again next year. At least that is what I had been told. I punched 10 times and the master still had the pencil between his fingers. Piece of cake, I said afterwards.

The next part of the test was to do a kata, a choreographed fighting dance. I had chosen Kanku Dai, which has two times as many movements as the other katas from which we could choose. No other student was silly enough to choose Kanku Dai. Only me. All the students did kata at the same time, and when they finished they could watch me. I have never chosen the easiest solution.

After finishing our katas the master chose another kata for each of the students to do. He chose the easiest for me. I was very grateful.

The next part of the test was Jiyu Ippon Kumite— fighting. I was by far the oldest and had to fight the next oldest. He was a big guy, approximately 40 years old. In the middle of the fight he kicked me very hard in my stomach. I was lifted off my feet into the air, but landed on the floor and made a quick counterattack.

My performance was acceptable, but it was only the first half of the fighting. To be accepted as a black belt in my home club, I had to fight all the other members in the club the next day. This was far worse than the weekend camp. The club members were sent against me two or three at a time with no break. One of them kicked me in the forehead while I was defending myself from another fighter's attack. I was bleeding and got a big bandage on the wound. Still, I continued fighting.

At last my sensei told all the members to attack me at one time. I think I fought against them for two minutes. There were 10 to 15 fighters, and I was happy when my sensei stopped the fight. He gave me the black belt. I was accepted.

Immediately after the test I went to the nearest hospital to have my forehead sewn. The doctor looked strangely at me when I entered in my white karate-gi with my new black belt. But I was very happy.

Why do I like karate? I am not very good at it, but it gives me a self-confidence I did not have before I started karate. When I was a boy I lived on the first floor with a lavatory in the basement. I was afraid of going down to the bathroom, and when I was there I was afraid to go back up to my apartment. I also had to fetch solid fuel from the dark basement, which I did not like either. I was afraid of the dark. I often dreamt that I was fighting with creatures in the basement.

When I grew up I got my own apartment with a stove.

Again I had to fetch solid fuel from the basement. I was not as afraid as when I was a boy, but I was a little afraid. And I still dreamed that I would have to fight against others.

Having done karate for ten years I am not afraid of the dark anymore. And I never fight when I dream.

Foods and fanaticism

I have been a vegetarian since 1963. I am sure it's one of the reasons I'm so healthy—at least as healthy as I think I am. I am not a fanatic. I can eat almost anything except meat. At the beginning I was a vegetarian because of my health, but today it's mostly because I respect the animals.

Except for my nearest family members, I have never told anyone that I am a vegetarian—until now. Not even at my work. I am not ashamed of being a vegetarian. But I have felt unpleasant when someone in a canteen announces with loud voice, "He is a vegetarian!" so that everybody could hear it. I don't think anybody would like to be called a "cadaver eater" Besides, I am not very fond of vegetables, and it would be more correct to call me "bread eater," but none have called me that. It's just not as interesting.

What is a fanatic? We all think we know what a fanatic is. The person who drinks two beers a day thinks that the man who drinks five beers a day is an alcoholic and that the person who doesn't touch alcohol is a fanatic. The person who runs two miles a day thinks that the person who runs a marathon is a fanatic and that the person who participates in an Ironman is crazy. The person who competes in an Ironman thinks that the person who participates in a tenfold Ironman must be kind of sick. But many people have completed a tenfold Ironman, and I am sure they do not consider themselves fanatics.

No man thinks of himself as a fanatic, whether it has to do with food or sports or another religion. But most people are quick to judge other persons as fanatics if they do not behave like themselves.

The Future

What are my expectations for the future in terms of training? I would like to continue doing squats, karate, yoga and jogging. I would like to do some weightlifting, especially using my legs. I would like to have more power in my weak leg. I will use my leg press machine more than I have done in the past. I will use it daily and put on more weights. I think that is the way to do it.

If I train the upper part of my body too much my weight will increase. A smaller upper body is better for my legs. It makes me run faster, and it makes me do karate better.

The bodybuilding experts say I should only train each muscle group one time each week. For example, I should only train my legs once a week. I understand that if someone lifts very heavy weights he or she needs time to recover. I remember when I got my leg press machine and wanted to see some quick results. Every week I added 22 more pounds (10 kg) of weight until it became too heavy for me. I have leg pressed 440 pounds (200 kg), but it was so heavy I could only press it if I yelled at the same time. I used all the muscles in my body, even the muscles around my heart, which hurt after pressing so much weight. I stopped this kind of training because I was afraid my heart might not be strong enough.

I want to lift weights every day. If I can add a little more weight to the barbell after a while I'll be happy. The most important thing is to continue training.

I am first dan black belt in Shotokan Karate. It is the lowest rank of the black belts. If I try to graduate to second dan I'll have to go through more testing. In one of these tests I will have to show I can kick at three adversaries without pausing between kicks: one in front, one at the right side and one behind. I will have to stand on my weak left leg and kick at the man in front of me first. Without touching the floor with my kicking leg I have to kick at the man on my right side. And then, still without touching the floor with the kicking leg, I have to kick to the rear. I cannot do these kicks. I have trained for 12 months on this exercise without getting much better. My left leg cannot keep me balanced while I am doing the three kicks.

I could ask permission to stand on my right leg instead and make the three kicks with my left leg. I could keep my balance standing on my right leg. But I have a problem of "dropping" my kicking leg when I kick to the rear. My kick to the rear cannot hurt a fly.

There is one good thing about this situation. I can stop thinking about graduating to second dan black belt.

Enough is enough.

I have always been interested in yoga. When I was younger I read lots of books about yoga: raja yoga, kriyayoga and hathayoga. I like to do my hathayoga exercises (headstand, shoulder stand, etc.). I will keep on doing those exercises.

I have tried meditation, but that isn't for me. Meditation can be many things. For example, meditating can mean to sit and repeat the same word or sentence for some time. Or, it can be not to think at all. To breathe in a special way (pranayama) can be meditation. You can sit in special positions when you meditate or lie down. I cannot sit in the lotus position. I like the different kinds of meditation, but experience tells me that I will be bored after some time.

One of my favorite things to do is to run with my dogs. They love to run with me. I run 2-4 miles (3-6 km) each day, with plenty of breaks. I want to run a little every day. It's no good to say, "Today I am tired. I will run tomorrow." Tomorrow I may be just as tired if not more so. And the day after tomorrow I may still be tired.

You can be tired even if you don't do anything. And before you know it, you have lost your good running habit.

Good habits are easily forgotten. The bad habits stick with you.

The Meaning of Life

What is the meaning of life? Perhaps that sounds too high-flown, but I cannot help asking the question.

People go to church to find the meaning of life. Others seek oriental religions if they are not satisfied with the answers they get from their priests. The most common opinion is that perfection of the soul must be the meaning of life, because when we die only the soul is left. So why try to make the body perfect if it vanishes when we die?

I believe that perfection of the body is just as important as perfection of the soul. I believe that soul and body are entangled more than we think. I think perfection of the body is an important step towards perfection of the soul.

Before I started jogging I often dreamt that somebody was chasing me, and I could not run to escape. Now I can run when I dream. Before I started karate I often dreamt I was fighting. Now I never fight when I dream. My psyche has become stronger when I dream.

I have read that to die feels the same as to dream—it feels like reality. And what is Purgatory, other than continuing with old inhibitions after death.

That is why I think the meaning of life is perfection of the soul through perfection of the body. I do not think it is important how strong, fast, beautiful, intelligent and spiritual we are. The important thing is that we feel strong, fast, beautiful, intelligent and spiritual, as well as feeling progress in our development. If we don't, we feel inferior, and an inferiority complex is like a weight around our necks pulling us down.

We are spiritual beings who have chosen to be on earth to develop toward perfection. Each of us must find our own way through life. And I think polio has helped me to find my way to contentment, peace and happiness.

My experience with polio has taught me to save my energy. I have learned to relax when my weak leg feels tired. I know the power will return quickly. I know my body, because I have been forced to listen to it. I know I have been lucky that polio didn't hurt me more than it did. I am grateful for the strength I possess.

May all people be filled with happiness and peace.